Welcome to ALADDIN QUIX!

If you are looking for fast, fun-to-read stories with colorful characters, lots of kid-friendly humor, easy-to-follow action, entertaining story lines, and lively illustrations, then **ALADDIN QUIX** is for you!

But wait, there's more!

If you're also looking for stories with tables of contents; word lists; about-the-book questions; 64, 80, or 96 pages; short chapters; short paragraphs; and large fonts, then **ALADDIN QUIX** is *definitely* for you!

ALADDIN QUIX: The next step between ready to reads and longer, more challenging chapter books, for readers five to eight years old.

Read all the ALADDIN QUIX books!

By Stephanie Calmenson

Our Principal Is a Frog!

Our Principal Is a Wolf!

Our Principal's in His Underwear!

Our Principal Breaks a Spell!

Royal Sweets
By Helen Perelman

Book 1: *A Royal Rescue*

Book 2: *Sugar Secrets*

Book 3: *Stolen Jewels*

A Miss Mallard Mystery
By Robert Quackenbush

Dig to Disaster

Texas Trail to Calamity

Express Train to Trouble

Stairway to Doom

Bicycle to Treachery

Gondola to Danger

Surfboard to Peril

Taxi to Intrigue

Little Goddess Girls
By Joan Holub and Suzanne Williams

Book 1: *Athena & the Magic Land*

Little GODDESS Girls

Athena & the Magic Land

**JOAN HOLUB
& SUZANNE
WILLIAMS**

ALADDIN QUIX

New York   London   Toronto   Sydney   New Delhi

For Alyson Heller, editorial goddess

—J. H. and S. W.

ALADDIN QUIX
Simon & Schuster Children's Publishing Division
1230 Avenue of the Americas, New York, New York 10020
First Aladdin QUIX paperback edition May 2019
Text copyright © 2019 by Joan Holub and Suzanne Williams
Illustrations copyright © 2019 by Yuyi Chen
Also available in an Aladdin QUIX hardcover edition.
All rights reserved, including the right of reproduction in whole or in part in any form.
ALADDIN and the related marks and colophon are trademarks of Simon & Schuster, Inc.
For information about special discounts for bulk purchases, please contact
Simon & Schuster Special Sales at 1-866-506-1949 or business@simonandschuster.com.
The Simon & Schuster Speakers Bureau can bring authors to your live event. For more information or to book an event contact the Simon & Schuster Speakers Bureau
at 1-866-248-3049 or visit our website at www.simonspeakers.com.
Designed by Karin Paprocki
The illustrations for this book were rendered digitally.
The text of this book was set in Archer Medium.
Manufactured in the United States of America 0621 OFF
2 4 6 8 10 9 7 5 3
The Library of Congress has cataloged the hardcover edition as follows:
Names: Holub, Joan, author. | Williams, Suzanne, 1953– author. | Chen, Yuyi (Artist), illustrator.
| Title: Athena & the magic land / by Joan Holub and Suzanne Williams ; illustrations by Yuyi
Chen. | Other titles: Athena and the magic land
Description: First Aladdin paperback edition. | New York : Aladdin, [2019] | Series: Little goddess
girls ; #1 | "Aladdin QUIX." | Summary: Young Athena is carried
by a storm to Mount Olympus, where she follows the
Hello Brick Road toward Sparkle City hoping Zeus will help her get home.
Identifiers: LCCN 2018031987 (print) | LCCN 2018037176 (eBook) |
ISBN 9781534431072 (eBook) | ISBN 9781534431058 (pbk) | ISBN 9781534431065 (hc)
Subjects: LCSH: Athena (Greek deity)—Juvenile fiction. | CYAC: Athena (Greek deity)—Fiction. |
Goddesses, Greek—Fiction. | Mythology, Greek—Fiction. | Fantasy.
Classification: LCC PZ7.H7427 (eBook) |
LCC PZ7.H7427 Asm 2019 (print) | DDC [E]—dc23
LC record available at https://lccn.loc.gov/2018031987

Cast of Characters

Athena (uh•THEE•nuh):
A brown-haired girl who travels to
magical Mount Olympus

Oliver (AH•liv•er): Athena's
puppy

Medusa (meh•DOO•suh):
A mean mortal girl with snakes
for hair, whose stare can turn
mortals to stone

Wiggle Warts (WIG•uhl WARTZ):
Medusa's pet snake in a game

Owlies (OWL·eez): Silly talking owls who live in magical Mount Olympus

Hestia (HESS·tee·uh): A small, winged Greek goddess who helps Athena

Zeus (ZOOSS): Most powerful of the Greek gods, who lives in Sparkle City and can grant wishes

Persephone (purr·SEFF·uh·nee): A girl with flowers and leaves growing in her hair and on her dress

Contents

1

Hello Brick Road!

Tap. Tap. Athena pushed the buttons on the tablet she held. The school bus came to a stop, and she hopped off. Without looking up from her tablet, she walked down the sidewalk. She lived in a white house on this block, with her mom, dad, and big sister.

Tap. Tap. Athena pushed more buttons. Happy Perky Pets was the best game ever! Even if she wasn't very good at it, it was still fun.

The goal was to get your pet to a happily-ever-after home. The pet she had chosen in the game was a cute little dog. He had white fur and a red collar. She'd named him **Oliver**. If only he were real!

Dogs were her very favorite animal. In fact, she had decorated her book bag with shiny dog-shaped stickers. Too bad her mom had said they couldn't get a real dog till she was older. Athena thought being eight was old enough!

Athena tapped the game button one more time.

Boink!

"Oh no!" A *boink* sound meant: *Oops! Start the game over and try again.*

"Ha! You lose." Athena looked behind her. It was **Medusa.** She

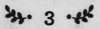

went to Athena's school and was never very nice to her. Or to anyone.

"So?" huffed Athena. She started walking faster. Medusa did too. Their houses were on this same street.

"You picked a *dog* for your pet?" Medusa teased. "BOR-ing! I picked a green snake. I named her **Wiggle Warts**."

Athena stared at her in surprise. *Eww!* She did not like snakes.

She looked down at her game

again. *Tap. Tap. Boink!* "Uh-oh, not again!" This time, lumpy brown **emojis** began appearing on the screen.

Medusa laughed. "Ha! Ha! You made doggie poo!" she said, pointing at the tablet.

Ugh. Medusa was right.

"Gotta go!" Athena said, speeding off. Medusa was always trying to **embarrass** her. That girl was a big meanie!

"Sorry, Oliver," Athena told the dog on her screen. "I wish I were better at this game. And we could go on lots of fun adventures. No meanie Medusa allowed."

Athena was only a few steps from her house now, but as she spoke, dark purple clouds appeared overhead. A bolt of lightning flashed across the sky! Thunder boomed.

A strong, sparkly wind whipped up and pulled the tablet from her hand. The tablet twirled around in the air like a spinning top, then fell to the grass. Before Athena could pick it up, the strange wind lifted her right off her feet! It blew her high into the sky. Athena whirled head over heels.

"What's *happening*?" Athena yelped.

Minutes later, the wind stopped. As fast as it had begun, the storm was over. And now Athena started falling! Down, down, down through the clouds she went.

Thump! She landed sitting in soft grass. Her book bag lay on the grass beside her.

Athena was okay. Except her shoes were gone.

So was her tablet. The wind had whisked them away!

"*Woof! Woof!*" Athena looked over to see a cute little white-haired dog. He looked . . . **familiar**.

The dog wagged his tail, ran over, and jumped into her lap. Athena read the name tag on his red collar: OLIVER.

Huh? Her dog from Happy Perky Pets was *real*?

She giggled when Oliver licked her cheek. Then he wiggled out of her lap and started barking again. **"Woof! Woof!"**

"What are you barking at, silly dog?" she asked. Looking around she saw three round owls sitting on a nearby bush. A yellow one, a pink one, and a blue one. They were staring at her.

"Whooo are you?" the owls asked.

Did those owls just talk? A bit alarmed, Athena jumped to her feet.

"I—I'm Athena," she replied. "Whooo—I mean, *who* are you?"

The owls blinked their big round eyes. "We are the **Owlies**," they announced.

"My name is Yellow Wing," said the yellow owl.

"I'm Pink Tail," said the pink owl.

"I'm Blue Feather," said the blue owl. She fluffed her feathers, which made Oliver bark again.

Athena patted the dog's head. "Shh! It's okay. They seem friendly." The dog licked her fingers. He was *sooo* cute!

She watched him trot off to sniff the grass by a tall street sign. "Hello Brick Road?" she said, reading the sign aloud.

"Hello," the sign answered.

Athena's eyes went wide. Not only did the owls talk, this sign talked too? Where had that wild wind dropped her, anyway?

This wasn't her street. Her street was gray and lined with houses. But Hello Brick Road was made of orange, blue, and pink bricks. And there weren't any houses along it. Only flowers, bushes, and trees.

"Wow! Where am I?" Athena wondered.

"In magical **Mount Olympus**, of course," replied a sweet voice.

"Who said that?" Athena

whipped around. There was a tiny glowing lady with wings. She was flying right in front of her nose!

2

Wiggly Hair

Athena stared at the tiny flying lady. "Are you a fairy?" she asked with excitement.

The Owlies hooted with laughter.

The tiny lady giggled. It made the glow around her **sparkle**. "I'm not a fairy. I'm a Greek **goddess**. My name is **Hestia**," she said.

Athena had never met a goddess before. She did not know much about them. Before she could ask Hestia if she was a special kind of goddess, they heard footsteps.

A girl about Athena's age came running up the brick road. She was chasing two golden birds that were flying just ahead of her.

"Come here. Right now!" the girl yelled at the birds.

Those birds did not listen. They

swooped and did loop-the-loops. Then they zoomed straight for Athena!

"Stop!" Athena tried to scoot out of their way, but she tripped and fell backward. ***Thonk!*** She landed with both legs in the air.

The birds kept coming. They dipped low. And then they slipped themselves onto her bare feet!

They weren't birds at all! They were golden sandals. Each with a white wing at the heel.

Athena stood up fast. *Whoosh!*

The sandals' golden straps wound up her ankles. They crisscrossed higher and higher. When the straps reached just below her knees, their ends tied themselves together.

"Give me those sandals. They're mine!" yelled the girl. Her hair was woven into many fat braids. And it was green.

Athena knew that voice. And that frowny face.

"Medusa? Is that you? Did the storm blow you to Mount

Olympus too?" Athena asked the girl.

"What storm? And how do you know my name?" demanded Medusa. Suddenly the green braids on her head began to wiggle. And hiss. And flick their red forked **tongues** at Athena.

Athena backed away. "Your braids. They're snakes!"

"Cute, right?" said Medusa. She patted the snakes fondly.

Medusa doesn't seem to know me, Athena thought. *And how*

did her hair turn into snakes?

Medusa took a step closer. "Who are you? Are you a goddess?"

"I'm Athena. From school, remember?" Had traveling to this magic land given Medusa snake hair? And made her forget the past?

Medusa frowned. "I don't know what you're talking about. Now give me those sandals. Or else."

"Don't do it," Hestia warned.

"Shoo, you!" Medusa flicked her hands at the tiny goddess. Hestia

zipped back and forth, staying out
of reach.

"Those sandals are magic,"
Hestia told Athena. "No one
knows all they can do. But if
Medusa gets them, she might find
out. And use their magic to make
trouble for Mount Olympus!"

"No I won't. Honest." Medusa sent Athena a fake-looking grin. "Let me hold the sandals. If I can figure out how they work, I'll make them grant you a wish."

Just then the light glowing around Hestia started to blink. "Oh dear, I have to go now," she said to Athena. "We'll meet again, soon, I promise." With that, she blinked out of sight.

"Last chance to take my offer," Medusa warned Athena.

"Home," Athena said in a rush.

"That's my wish. I want to go home."

"Woof! Woof!" barked Oliver. He ran over to Athena.

"With my dog, Oliver," she added quickly, hugging him.

"Sure. No problem," Medusa replied. "But first hand over the sandals."

"Okay," Athena agreed. She was worried that Medusa was up to no good. But Athena had to get back home. She didn't belong in this magic land and couldn't stay. She missed her family!

Athena bent down to untie the sandal straps. She tugged and tugged at the ties, but they wouldn't **budge**. "I can't undo them!" she said in surprise.

"Let me try." Medusa reached for the straps. One of them undid itself enough to smack her hand away. The other straps unwound and grabbed her leg. *Oomph!* She fell on her bottom.

The Owlies hooted.

As the straps retied themselves,

Medusa leaped up. Looking angry, she wagged a finger at Athena. "Trick me, will you? Well, you'll be sorry!"

"Grr!" growled Oliver. He bared his teeth at Medusa.

Medusa backed off. "And keep your little dog away from me, or he'll be sorry too!" Her snakes hissed in agreement.

With that, Medusa and her snakes disappeared in a puff of green smoke!

"Oh no!" wailed Athena. "How will I get home now?"

"**Zeus**!" the owl named Yellow Wing told her.

"Whooo, I mean, *who* is Zeus?" Athena asked.

"The king of all the **gods** on Mount Olympus!" explained Blue Feather.

"No problem is too big for the super-duper powerful Zeus to fix," added Pink Tail.

"Where do I find him?" Athena asked eagerly.

The Owlies fluttered their feathers. "At the top of Mount Olympus. In Sparkle City."

"How do I get there?" Athena asked.

"On the Hello Brick Road," said Blue Feather.

Athena looked down the long road made of orange, blue, and pink bricks. "All by myself? What if Medusa comes back?"

"As long as you stay on the road, she won't have any power to hurt you," Pink Tail assured her.

Then the street sign piped up again. "Besides, you'll make new friends on the Hello Brick Road.

If you see a friendly face just say hello."

"Time for a nap," Yellow Wing hooted. The three Owlies flew back to their bush and waved good-bye to Athena.

When Athena wished for an adventure, she'd never imagined anything like this. It looked like that wish was coming true. Would her going-home wish come true too?

Athena picked up her book bag. "Come on, Oliver. Let's go find Zeus!"

3

Stuck in the Muck

Athena skipped happily along the Hello Brick Road. Oliver trotted beside her. There were bunches of colorful flowers planted on both sides of the path. At the far end of the road ahead, she could see tiny rainbow-colored sparkles. That was Sparkle City!

"Too bad Sparkle City is waaay up at the top of Mount Olympus," she told Oliver. "It's going to take forever to get there. I wish there were a faster way."

At Athena's words, the wings on her sandals began flapping. The sandals lifted her a few inches off the ground. They flew her sideways. **_Whoosh!_** They zigzagged her backward. _Swoosh!_

"Oof!" She brushed against

a flower bush as tall as she was. She spun her arms, trying not to fall. Not again! This was almost as bad as being tossed around by that storm.

"Hey! Stop, you silly sandals!" Athena shouted.

Right away the wings stopped flapping. They floated her lower. Finally the sandals rested on the brick road once more. But now their wings sagged. It seemed that she'd embarrassed them with her yelling. And maybe hurt their feelings too.

Athena knew how that felt. It's how Medusa made her feel all the time. Mostly when she teased Athena about how bad she was at playing Happy Perky Pets.

"Thank you for trying to help me go faster," she told the sandals kindly. "It's not your fault I'm not good at flying. I probably just need more practice." Hearing this, the wings perked up, starting to flap again.

"Wait! Not right now though. Maybe later," Athena said quickly.

She wasn't ready to try flying again quite yet!

"Mmm. What's that sweet smell?" she said, sniffing the air. The sandals had taken her close to a big flower bush.

What a pretty bush, she thought. It grew many kinds of flowers. There were colorful daisies, roses, and lilies all over it. She reached out to sniff a perfect red rose.

"Stop!" shouted a girl's voice.

Athena jumped back. "Who said that?"

"Me!" A girl's face popped up from the top of the bush. She had daisies growing in her hair! And she wore a cute dress made of leaves and flowers.

The two girls stared at each other. Then Athena remembered what the Hello Brick Road sign had told her about making friends.

"Hello. I'm Athena," she said to the girl.

"I'm **Persephone**." The girl grinned.

"Are you a girl or a flower bush?" Athena asked.

Persephone laughed. "I'm both." Then she frowned. "And I'm stuck in the **muck**."

"Oh. Is there a way I can help?"

Athena stepped closer to her.

"Stay back!" Persephone yelped. She held up both hands, keeping Athena away.

Uh-oh! Maybe this girl didn't want to be friends after all?

Persephone sighed. It made her leaves flutter. "I have a bad case of **bad luck-itis**," she explained. "I wouldn't want you to catch it. You see, horrible things are always happening to me. Like today. I came into this garden to help some droopy flowers feel better. Instead I grew roots."

She lifted the hem of her leafy flower dress. Athena stared in surprise. Persephone's legs ended in tangled roots that went down under the ground.

"I can't move. See?" Persephone tried to pull her roots out of the dirt. She tugged on one leg and then the other. The roots didn't budge.

"That *is* bad luck," agreed Athena. If only she could help! She stared at Persephone's roots.

"Woof!"

Athena looked over at her new dog. He was sniffing and pawing at a beetle in the grass. That gave her the perfect idea.

"Come, Oliver!" she called out. When he dashed over, she pointed to the dirt around Persephone's roots. "Dig, boy!"

Oliver wagged his tail. Then he started to dig. Dirt flew as his front paws dug deep. Before long Persephone was free!

Persephone leaped from the garden to stand on the road. Her

roots magically became feet again! She wiggled her bright-green painted toenails in delight. She gave Athena a big smile. "Thanks."

Persephone's leafy, flowery dress rustled as she bent to pat Oliver. "And thank you, too," she said. She laughed as he tried to give her kisses.

She straightened and pointed to some droopy flowers at the side of the road. "I wish my luck were better," she said with a sigh. "Then I could use it to help all plants grow strong and beautiful. Wouldn't that be great?"

"Hmm." A new idea came to Athena. She pointed at the rainbow sparkles in the distance. "Want to go to Sparkle City? I'm on my way there to see Zeus," she told Persephone. "He's the super-duper powerful king of the gods. I'm going to ask him to help me get back home. Maybe you can ask for the gift of good luck."

Persephone's big green eyes twinkled with excitement. "That's an **awesome** idea. With good luck, I could help the flowers!"

The two girls high-fived. "Onward to Sparkle City!" they shouted. Then they skipped down the road. Oliver trotted along behind them.

That street sign was right, thought Athena. *It* was *easy to make new friends on the Hello Brick Road!*

4

Talking Trees

Athena and Persephone came to a forest.

Athena's tummy rumbled. "I'm hungry."

"Me too," said Persephone. Then she pointed ahead. "Look! **Plums**!"

Some fruit trees stood in the forest. They were behind a low white fence at the side of the road.

Both girls stared at the plums. Then they looked at each other. "Are you thinking what I'm thinking?" asked Athena.

"We'll have those plums for lunch!" Persephone said.

"Stay," Athena told Oliver.

The girls climbed over the white fence. They ran to the fruit trees. They stood on tiptoe to reach the purple plums growing on their lower branches.

Whoosh! The branches began to sway wildly.

"Who is there, picking on us?" demanded a tree.

"Looks like two troublemaking mini monsters!" another plum tree replied.

Athena jumped in surprise.

"Oops! We didn't mean any harm," she told the trees.

Persephone nodded. "We're just hungry. And your plums look so yummy."

Frowning, the first plum tree crossed its branches over its trunk. The other trees did the same, as if to **protect** their plums.

"Have you no manners? Now bow and ask us for them **politely**!" the first tree demanded.

"Oh! Of course. Sorry," said

Athena. Though it made her feel a bit silly, she bowed to the tree. "Can we *please* have some plums?"

"NO!" shouted the fruit trees. They were so loud that the girls put their hands over their ears.

The first plum tree pointed a fingerlike twig at them. "Let's just see how you mini monsters like being picked on."

Athena felt something wrap around her waist. A branch! The trees scooped up both girls and began to twirl them like **batons**.

"I'm getting d-d-dizzy!" yelled Athena, dropping her book bag.

"Yeah! My head is sp-sp-sp-spinning!" yelled Persephone.

Hearing the girls, Oliver sprang into action. He squeezed under the fence and ran toward them, barking.

"No, Oliver. G-g-go back!" called Athena. "Before the trees grab you, too!" Luckily Oliver was good at **dodging** their branches. But his barking wasn't helping at all. It only made the trees madder!

Now they began to juggle. The girls were tossed up in the air from tree to tree. As easily as if they were, well, plums!

"This is my fault. I told you I have bad luck-itis." Persephone let out an unhappy laugh. "Sorry, I know this isn't funny. Sometimes I laugh when I'm upset."

Laugh? *Wait a second!* That gave Athena an idea.

"Hey, trees!" she called out. "You know what? I think you're the ones with bad manners. And we're not

mini monsters. We're actually"—
she held up both hands and wiggled
her fingers—"*tickle* monsters!"

Athena began to tickle the trunk
of the tree that was holding her.
Catching on, Persephone did the
same to her tree.

The trees started giggling.
"Ooh! Eee! Ooh!" They
wiggled. They wobbled and
shook. This made some of their
plums drop to the ground.

Persephone and Athena kept on
tickling. Finally the trees laughed

so hard that they let go of the girls.

Athena and Persephone fell

onto a pile of

soft leaves. Quickly they stuffed

as many plums as they could grab

into Athena's book bag. They ran for the road. Oliver **scampered** close behind them. He squeezed back under the fence as they climbed over.

Giggling themselves, now, the girls raced down the road. When they were well beyond the trees, they slowed to walk and eat their yummy plums.

It wasn't long until the Hello Brick Road came to a dead end. Only a grassy field stretched before the girls now. All across it, large animal-shaped stones stood in rows like soldiers. There were life-size monkeys, deer, wolves, bears, giraffes, and more!

Athena pointed to a hill in the field beyond the statues. "Maybe the road starts again on the other side of that hill."

When the girls began to tiptoe past the weird statues toward the hill, they heard shuffling noises.

"Uh-oh," Persephone whispered. She pointed to a stone bear up ahead of them. "Did it just move?"

Athena's eyes got big. "Yes," she whispered. In fact the animal statues were *all* moving now . . . and coming right toward them!

The statues came closer. And closer.

"It's my bad luck-itis again!" Persephone exclaimed. "We're surrounded!"

5

Stone Statues

The stone statues began to march in a circle around Athena and Persephone. *Stomp. Stomp. Stomp.* As they marched, they chanted a song. It was a *rock* concert!

"Once we were animals. Now we are stone.

*"Changed by a **mortal** girl perched on a throne.*

"Each one of us she has skillfully trapped.

"Now it's your turn to be magically zapped."

Persephone gulped. "Zapped? That doesn't sound good."

"Changed by a *mortal* girl?" said Athena. "But mortals are human. And humans don't have magic zapping powers. Maybe this zap-girl is some kind of special *evil* mortal?"

"We're doomed!" Persephone wailed.

Just then hissing sounds filled the air around them. The stone statues stopped marching, and everyone looked up.

High in the sky were huge green letters that spelled out one word:

Medusa

Athena **gasped**.

"Who is Medusa?" Persephone asked.

"A mean girl with snake hair," Athena explained quickly. "I think she must have zapped a bunch of *real* animals and turned them into those stone ones. Then she made them her army!"

Now the green letters broke apart and wiggled around to form a new word: SANDALS.

"Oh, I forgot to tell you. Medusa wants my sandals," Athena added.

Both girls peeked down at Athena's golden-sandaled feet.

"Well, they are supercute," said Persephone.

Athena shrugged. "But even more important, they can fly. A goddess named Hestia told me Medusa might use them to make trouble for Mount Olympus."

Persephone got a determined look on her face. "Then we can't let Medusa get them!"

All of a sudden they heard a terrible cackle. **"Eee-heh-heh!"**

It was Medusa! For some reason she was bald now. She glanced up at the green letters high above them. She snapped her fingers.

"Wiggle Warts!" she called.

At her command the green letters broke apart into long squiggles. They shot down from the sky. Each had a flicking red tongue!

Athena blinked in surprise. Those squiggles were Medusa's snakes! Now they wiggled back to her head and became her hair again.

"Wow! Skywriting snake hair!" said Persephone.

Medusa snapped her fingers once more. The stone animals moved aside, and she stepped closer to Athena. "Give me the sandals," she demanded.

Athena shook her head. "I already tried, remember? They won't come off."

Medusa glared at her. "Then prepare to be zapped into stone!"

The wings on Athena's sandals fluttered in fear. The daisies on

Persephone's head drooped with fright.

Pink Tail the owl had said that Medusa couldn't hurt Athena if she stayed on the road. But she and Persephone had crossed into the field. Now Medusa could spell T-R-O-U-B-L-E for them!

Athena thought fast. "Wait! I'm wearing the sandals."

"So?" asked Medusa.

"So if you zap me into stone, the sandals will also turn to stone," explained Athena. "And they will be too heavy to fly."

Medusa pointed a green finger at Persephone. "Oh yeah? Then maybe I'll turn your flower girl friend to stone instead."

"Um, no, thanks," Persephone said.

Thinking fast, Athena grabbed Persephone's hand. "If you turn Persephone to stone while we're holding hands, I'll turn to stone too. And so will the sandals!"

Medusa frowned. Her snakes flicked their tongues and hissed.

Oliver barked at them. **"Woof! Woof!"**

"Shush, you silly dog! I'm trying to think," grumped Medusa. Then she smiled. It was an extra-mean smile. *Evil*, in fact!

Medusa squinted her eyes at Oliver. ***Zap!***

Suddenly Oliver sat down and stopped barking. He didn't move. And he wasn't white anymore. He was gray!

Athena tried to pet him. His fur was stiff, hard, and smooth. He'd

been turned to stone! "Nooo! What have you done?" she wailed.

Medusa just cackled. **"Eee-heh-heh!"**

"Please change him back," begged Athena.

"Nope. Not unless you find a way to give me the sandals," said Medusa.

"Oh, Athena! I brought you bad luck again!" groaned Persephone.

"No! It's not your fault," said Athena. She had to think of a way to fix things!

Her gaze fell on the book bag she held. It was covered with stickers. Stickers as shiny as mirrors. *Hmm*. She had tricked those plum trees. Could she trick Medusa, too?

Athena crossed her fingers behind her back. "Okay, Medusa. If you zap Oliver back to life, I'll give you the sandals. They listened to me a while ago when I told them to stop flying. So if I ask them to leave my feet, I think they will. Then you could grab them."

"I like your plan. It's a deal!" said Medusa.

Athena went to stand beside the stone bear. Then she said to

Medusa, "But *before* you can have the sandals, I want you to zap this stone bear back into a real one. That's to prove you'll be able to change Oliver back when it's time."

"Sure," Medusa said eagerly. She squinted at the stone bear. **Zap!**

At the exact same moment, Athena held up her book bag. She tilted it so the zap hit one of the shiny animal stickers instead of the bear.

The shiny sticker acted like a mirror. Medusa's zap bounced off it and hit Oliver. *Bling!* Glittery sparkles whooshed around the little dog.

"Woof! Woof!" Athena's trick worked! Oliver turned into a real dog again.

She scooped him up in her arms. "Run!" she yelled to Persephone.

"Hey!" Medusa shouted as the two girls took off toward the hill. "Did you just do magic? You *are* goddesses, aren't you?"

Athena and Persephone just kept on running.

Behind them Medusa shook her fist. "You just wait! I'll get you next time. Those winged sandals will be mine!"

6

Goddesses

As Athena had hoped, the Hello
Brick Road started again on
the other side of the hill. Soon
the girls were back safe on the
orange, blue-green, and pink
road.

"Think we really could be goddesses?" Persephone asked as they walked along.

Athena thought it over. "We're in a magic land. Anything is possible. I know! I'll try zapping something to find out." She pointed a finger at some moss hanging in a tree. "Abracadabra. Presto change-o!"

Nothing happened.

"Hmm. I'll try an eye zap, like Medusa did," said Persephone. She squinted her eyes at the moss. But nothing happened.

"Maybe we need to say what we want the moss to become," said Athena. She pointed her finger at the moss. "Presto change-o into cake!" she commanded.

Persephone licked her lips. "Ooh, good one! Cake. Yum."

But instead of turning into cake, the moss began to glow. Then a tiny winged goddess sprang from it.

Persephone clapped. "Even better than cake. You magicked a fairy here!"

Athena laughed. "No, that's Hestia, the goddess I told you about."

"You didn't magic me here," Hestia explained. "I came on my own as I promised. I only have a few moments before I blink away, so listen up."

The two girls went quiet.

"More adventures await you on your trip to Sparkle City," Hestia told them. "Troubles, too. Along the way you will find a beautiful shell. Tap on it three times, and it

will open. Inside you will find—"
She stopped speaking as her glow
began to blink.

"Wait! What will we find inside?"
Athena asked.

"And what kind of troubles await
us?" asked Persephone. "More
terrible tree troubles? Medusa
madness? Snake scares?"

Hestia's voice became as faint
as her glow. "Just remember this:
Wherever you roam, the best
place is home."

Pop! She disappeared again.

"Wherever you roam, the best place is home," Athena repeated softly. She looked at Persephone. "That's why we've got to get to Sparkle City. Zeus will help me get back home!"

"And turn my bad luck to good luck!" added Persephone.

Athena stared ahead at the top of Mount Olympus. It gleamed with the rainbow sparkles of Sparkle City. Though Medusa danger still hung over them, for now, they were safe. Plus they had each other—and Oliver!

She smiled at Persephone. "What are we waiting for? Let's go!"

The new friends linked arms and began to happily skip down the Hello Brick Road, with Oliver right by their side.

Word List

awesome (AWE•sum): Great

bad luck-itis (bad luck•I•tiss):
A made-up kind of bad luck

batons (buh•TAHNZ): Long
sticks twirled by drum majors

budge (BUHJ): Move

dodging (DAH•jing): Moving
out of the way

emojis (ee•MO•jees): Tiny
pictures that show an idea or
feeling

embarrass (em•BARE•uss):
Cause someone to feel ashamed,
uncomfortable, or anxious

familiar (fuh•MIL•yur):
Someone or something that
seems well-known

gasped (GASPED): Took a
surprised breath

goddess (GOD•ess): A girl or
woman with magic powers in
Greek mythology

gods (GODZ): Boys or men with
magic powers in Greek mythology

Greece (GREES): A country on

the continent of Europe

Greek mythology (GREEK mith•AH•luh•jee): Stories people in **Greece** made up long ago to explain things they didn't understand about their world

mortal (MOR•tuhl): A human

Mount Olympus (MOWNT oh•LIHM•pus): Tallest mountain in Greece

muck (MUCK): Dirt

plums (PLUMS): Sweet, round fruits that are purple, red, or yellow when ripe

politely (po•LYTE•lee): Using good manners

protect (pro•TEKT): Keep safe

scampered (SKAM•perd): Ran quickly

sparkle (SPAR•kul): Shine bright

tongues (TUNGS): Tasting organs found inside the mouth of people (or animals!)

Questions

1. Do you think it would be fun to be a goddess or a god? Why? Or why not?

2. If you were a goddess or a god, what would your magic power be?

3. If you found out you were a goddess, who would you tell?

4. Medusa says things to hurt Athena's feelings. Has anyone ever done this to you?

5. Why do you think Athena and

Persephone become friends so quickly? What makes a good friendship, in your opinion?

6. Do you think Zeus will help Athena and Persephone? How?

7. What adventures do you think Athena and Persephone will have?

8. What do you think will happen in the next book with the shell Hestia mentions in the last chapter of this book?

Authors' Note

Some of the ideas in the Little Goddess Girls books come from Greek mythology.

Athena was the Greek goddess of wisdom. That means she was super smart! If there was an emoji for Athena, it might be an owl. Because owls are symbols of smartness.

If there was an emoji for Medusa, it might be a snake. In Greek mythology she has snakes on her head instead of hair. Medusa could turn mortals to stone just by looking at them!

We also borrowed a few ideas from *The Wonderful Wizard of Oz* by L. Frank Baum. In that book there is a Yellow Brick Road. In Little Goddess Girls, you'll find a Hello Brick Road.

We hope you enjoy reading the Little Goddess Girls books!

—*Joan Holub and Suzanne Williams*